LAURENT DE BRUNHOFF

BABAR
AND THE
PROFESSOR

Translated from the French by Olive Jones

METHUEN CHILDREN'S BOOKS
LONDON

Have you read
these other books by
Jean de Brunhoff:

The Story of Babar
Babar's Travels
Babar the King
Babar at Home
Babar and Father Christmas
Babar's Friend Zephir
?

And these by
Laurent de Brunhoff:

Babar's Castle
Picnic at Babar's
Babar and that Rascal Arthur
Babar's Fair
Babar's Visit to Bird Island
Babar's Birthday Surprise
?

First published under the title "Babar et le Professeur Grifaton"
First published in Great Britain 1972 by Methuen Children's Books Ltd,
11 New Fetter Lane, London EC4
Copyright © 1956 by Librairie Hachette
English translation © 1972 by Methuen Children's Books Ltd
Printed by Casterman S.A., Belgium
SBN 416 08890 2

At Celesteville, the town of the elephants,
King Babar and Queen Celeste live happily with
their children, Pom, Flora and Alexander
and their cousin Arthur.
One day Babar received a letter from his friend
the Old Lady. "Listen to this," he told the children.
"Dear Babar, I miss you all very much
and hope to visit you soon.
My brother, Professor Grifaton, will probably be
coming with me, and his two grandchildren,
Colin and Nadine. I can't tell you
how happy I shall be to see you again."
"This is very good news," said Babar,
and the children shouted, "Hurrah!"

The great day came and everyone joined in welcoming
the visitors. Professor Grifaton had heard so much
about Babar and Celeste that he was delighted to meet

them at last. Babar and Celeste kissed the Old Lady.
The children greeted their new friends. And all the
elephants were interested in the Professor's car.

Professor Grifaton
took
the children
with him
to catch
butterflies.

He taught them the names of those he put in his bag.
Pom couldn't resist blowing on
a beautiful yellow butterfly just as
Professor Grifaton was going to catch it. The Professo
was cross but Colin thought it a great joke.

When they got back from their walk they gathered
in the Professor's room. He showed them where
he kept his butterflies. "As you see," he told Pom,
"the box is made of plastic and can be taken to pieces.
The holes at the side let the air in."
Colin, on all fours on the carpet, looked
at a book of butterfly photographs,
while Arthur admired the microscope, but without
daring to touch it. Suddenly Nadine, who had
stayed outside in the garden, called through the window.
"Alexander! Pom!
Come quickly! I've just made
an extraordinary discovery!"

Nadine led them to the entrance of a cave
which was partly hidden behind some branches.
The little elephants were very excited and decided
to set up house there. Pom brought some big cushions which
the Old Lady lent him to make the place comfortable.
By the light of lanterns they all set to work.

When everything was ready in the cave, the children
invited Babar and Celeste and their friends. With the help
of the Old Lady they had prepared a sumptuous meal,
with plenty of cakes. Greedy Arthur
took a whole plate of éclairs just for himself!

Then Nadine and her friends disappeared
for a few minutes behind a curtain. They came back

dressed up in theatrical costumes
they had found in cupboards in the Palace of Pleasure!

When Alexander went into the dressing room to change
his clothes, he thought he'd do something clever.
"I'd like to see where this tunnel goes," he decided.
He went cautiously into it, taking the lantern.
After twisting several times
the passage opened out
and there was a big hole.
Alexander
leaned over.

He tried
to see to the bottom
and—oh, goodness!
he slipped, rolled and fell.
The lantern broke and he was
in darkness. Alexander cried
and called .... At last the others
came hurrying with electric torches.
Arthur slid down into the hole and
comforted Alexander. Podular threw
a rope to the little elephant and
hauled him gently to the top again.

The children took off their costumes, and everyone
went back into the garden. "This cave
strikes me as very interesting," said Professor Grifaton.
"Don't you think, Babar, that we should
explore the passages?"
"That's a fine idea!" said Babar. "Let's organise
a proper expedition."
"Yes, do let's!" cried Arthur.
"First thing tomorrow," said Cornelius, "I'll start
getting together equipment, and all the things we need."
"Good," said Babar. "And you, my dear Professor,
should go and see my friend
Podular the sculptor, who is
an amateur spelaeologist."

Next day Babar gathered together his team
to descend into the cave.
This of course included Babar himself and Arthur,
Podular the sculptor, Olur the mechanic
and Dr Capoulosse, whose presence
was a very necessary precaution.
Dressed in waterproof suits
and wearing safety helmets
the elephants went into the cave.
Colin and Nadine waved goodbye to them.

They discovered
an underground river and glided along in their rubber dingh
In the darkness, among the stalactites, they saw
a very old statue of a mammoth. Arthur was fascinated.

Carried along by the underground river,
the dinghies came out
on the lake at Celesteville!
"So you can get into the cave from the lake!"
cried the Professor.
"That's a most exciting discovery!"
He went to see the harbourmaster at Celesteville
and stayed talking to him for a long time.
The elephants wondered what he was planning.
"Professor Grifaton is full of ideas.
What's he up to now?" they asked.
Well, the Professor's plan was to make a boat!

RIVER BOAT

Invented and Designed
by Proffessor Grifaton

DRIVEN BY ATOMIC POWER WITH
LATERAL PADDLE WHEELS

KEY

1. Captain's cabin and Bridge
2. Dining Saloon
3. Bar and Library
4. Dance Hall
5. Galley
6. Refrigerator
7. Pantry
8. Sick-bay
9. Photographic Studio
10. Shop
11. Cloakroom
12. Engines
13. Hold
14. A. Deck
15. B. Deck
16. Paddle Wheel

RIVER BOAT
TRIP ROUND THE LAKE 10 p
EXTRA TO SEE THE CAVES 5 p
NEXT TRIP 2.30 pm

ICES

In due course the river boat was ready for its first trip. "Well, you've succeeded with your plan, Professor," said Babar. "I think all the elephants

are very happy about it.'' Everyone hurried on board
as the hooter sounded and the sailors prepared to
cast off. But where had the children gone?

Too late! The boat
has gone. The barrier
is shut until tomorrow.

A sailor who saw
how upset the children
were, told them:

"In five minutes the boat
will go under the bridge.
Run! You'll catch it!"

The children raced
on to the bridge, and
got there just in time.

Arthur leaned over
the parapet, and waved
frantically to the boat.

The captain saw them
from the wheelhouse, and
gave the order to stop.

A rope ladder
was thrown from the boat,
and they scrambled down.

They all threw themselves into the arms of Babar
and Celeste—but they were rather proud
of their escapade. "What happened?" asked Celeste.
"I told you clearly you hadn't time to go
off on your bicycles before the boat left."
But the children were too out of breath
to answer.
Under the canvas which shaded them from the sun
they rested their elbows on the rail
and watched the water slipping under the boat.
"What a wonderful outing this is,"
said the Old Lady to the Professor.

When they reached the underground river
the boat drew alongside a landing-stage.
The passengers disembarked
into motor-boats. But Cornelius and the Old Lady
thought the damp air of the cave might be bad
for their rheumatism. "Goodbye! Don't do anything
silly!" they said. "Toot, toot! Let's go! cried Arthur.
Babar switched on the headlight of his motor-boat.

The headlights lit up the cave which seemed

immense. It was indeed a mammoth's palace!

An hour later the river boat came in sight
of the harbour at Celesteville.

"Three cheers for the river boat! Three cheers for
Professor Grifaton!" cried the elephants crowded
at the quayside, each edging forward for a better view.

The young ones climbed on the shoulders of their parents
or on motor cars. "Tomorrow we'll get here early
and get a good place on the boat," said one of them.
"I shall be here first." "No, I shall," said another.

That evening, in the Palace of Pleasure, Cornelius
decorated Professor Grifaton, and pinned on his chest
the Grand Elephant Order of Celesteville.
The ceremony took place in the presence of King Babar
and Queen Celeste.
At home, the children, in their pyjamas, were watching
the scene on television with the Old Lady.
They were very excited and applauded loudly.